For Nicholas and Francesca

A Lion for Niccolby

SUSAN SACHER PHILIPSON

Illustrated by Giovanni Guarcello

Pantheon Books

The night was still, the moon was high
And clouds were scudding 'cross the sk[y]
But 'neath a weeping willow tree
A lion sighed in misery.

For he was striped from head to toe,
And only just a month ago
The jungle court demanded he
Remove his stripes immediately.

He said that he would gladly try,
But as the days went rushing by
The lion soon began to fear
His stripes would never disappear.

An elder member of his clan
Had painted him a shade of tan,
But to the lion's great dismay,
It rained and washed the paint away.

And so he said that he would wear
A special coat of camel's hair,
But soon the coat began to shed
And stripes appeared upon his head.

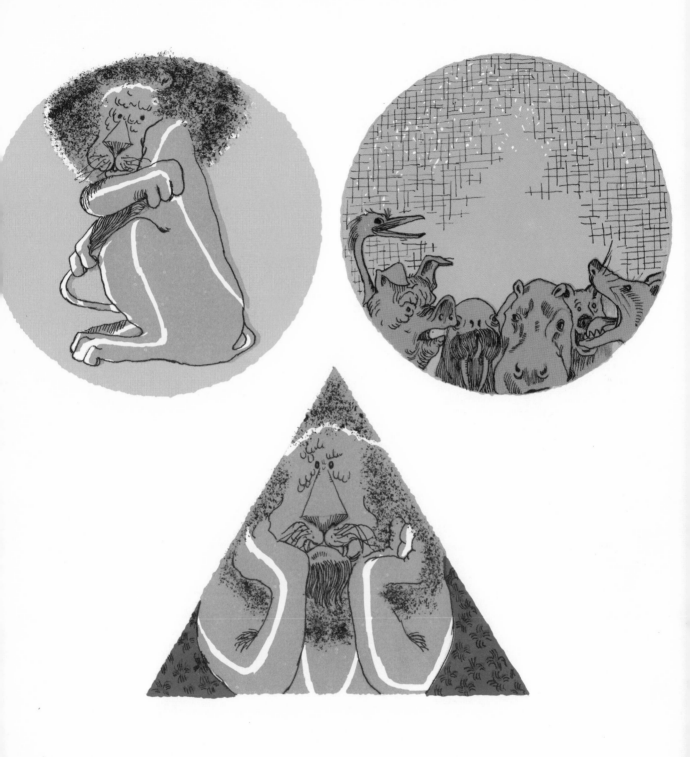

"Unlucky day that I was born,"
The lion whimpered, all forlorn.
"My family even thinks me strange
And yet, I simply cannot change."

This very night, at half-past nine,
The jungle court sat down to dine,
And afterward the grizzly bear
Got up and took the speaker's chair.

"Garuuumph!" he said ("Garuuuumph" again)
And loudly cleared his throat——"AHEM!
It's time the lion should be told
We think his stripes are far too bold.

"Indeed, we've never had a king
With such a silly covering!"
The others all began to frown:
"The lion must give up his crown!"

He thought his heart would surely break,
But for his noble family's sake
He sadly left his old domain
And climbed aboard a passing train.

Before he'd traveled very far
He chose to leave the baggage car,
And greeting people with a smile,
He gaily sauntered up the aisle.

The passengers were pale with fright,
Convinced that he would take a bite,
But one old lady thought him sweet
And asked if he would like a seat.

Now, while the others gaped and gawked,
The lady and the lion talked
And got along so famously
They even had a cup of tea.

But when the train conductor saw
There was no ticket in his paw,
He grabbed him by his shaggy mane
And told the men to stop the train.

"I'm sorry, sir, you'll have to go.
You cannot ride for free, you know.
Besides," he said, "it seems to me
A zoo is where you ought to be."

So puffing hard with all his might,
He wound a rope around him tight,
And presently, when he was through,
He notified the city zoo.

The lion spent a peaceful night,
But when the sun was warm and bright,
He heard the tigers bickering,
And some were even snickering!

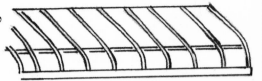

"Now isn't he a clown," they said,
"With all those stripes upon his head."
"You'd think that he would be ashamed,"
The water buffalo exclaimed.

The monkeys on the jungle gym
Believed his stripes were just a whim,
But angry was the crocodile,
Who showed a most ferocious smile.

"Ignore him," said the kangaroo.
"I quite agree," replied the gnu,
"As anyone can plainly see,
He simply wants our flattery."

"He's really too ridiculous,"
Remarked the hippopotamus,
Who gave his tail a mighty thud
And wallowed deeper in the mud.

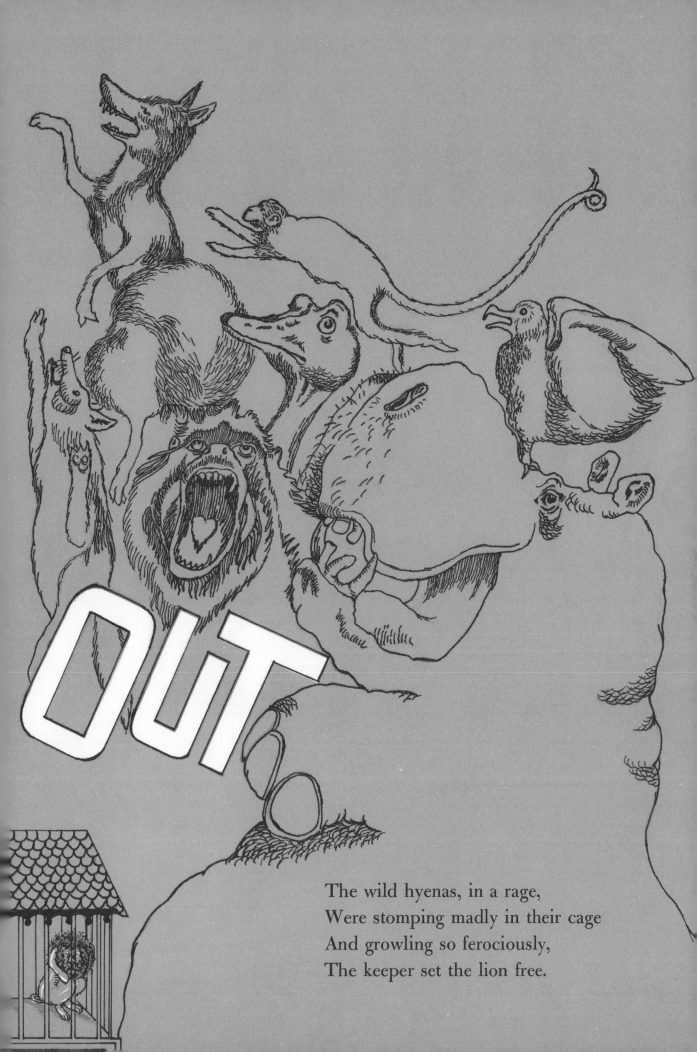

The wild hyenas, in a rage,
Were stomping madly in their cage
And growling so ferociously,
The keeper set the lion free.

Sadly wond'ring what to do,
He padded up Fifth Avenue
Until he came upon a store
That had a notice on the door:

LION NEEDED DESPERATELY
PLEASE APPLY TO MR. GEE

And feeling slightly happier,
He went to see the manager.

They hired him that very day
To be their center floor display,
But he was cautioned not to roar
Or they would take him off the floor.

And so he sat in this disguise
And never even blinked his eyes
Or made the slightest sound at all
Except a sneeze (and that was small).

Until a girl, all pink and frail,
Decided she would pull his tail,
And when he frowned unhappily,
She promptly kicked him in the knee.

Now, when they heard his mighty roar,
The people shopping in the store
Began to flee in great alarm
Despite his look of toyish charm.

And when he saw them rushing out,
The manager began to shout:
"Now look what you have gone and don
You've spoiled everybody's fun!"

The lion hung his head in shame:
"But, sir," he said, "I'm not to blame.
Allow me just this one mistake
And I will prove I *can* be fake."

"Indeed you *are*!" the owner cried.
"A lion should be dignified,
But dignity you surely lack.
Get out at once, *and don't come back*."

How sad he felt, and all alone,
As homeless as a rolling stone.
That evening, when the sky was dark,
He wandered through the children's park.

He didn't close his weary eyes
Until the sun began to rise.
At last, beneath a willow tree,
The lion slept contentedly.

Drifting . . . drifting . . . lazily,
He floated in a reverie
Where he beheld a lovely sight,
An island shimm'ring in the night.

And when he landed, suddenly
He heard a sweet Calliope,
And following its lovely call,
He found the strangest thing of all:

Beneath a tent a pink gazelle
Was prancing on a carrousel.
Round and round and round went he,
"Come on," he cried, "the ride is free!"

And animals from every side
Came galloping to have a ride.
Two red elephants were there,
And one giraffe with curly hair . . .

A tiger wearing glasses, too,
And by his side a zebra who
Was munching on a honey sweet,
A pair of gaiters on his feet.

Behind them was a silver fox
Who wore a pair of checkered socks,
And last of all a tabby cat
In knickers and a derby hat.

And to the lion's great surprise,
The carrousel began to rise
Until it vanished out of sight
Behind a veil of smoky light.

The island too had disappeared,
And when at last the mist had cleared
The lion's face lit up with joy,
For there he saw a little boy.

"How do you do, Your Majesty?
My name is Alex Niccolby."
And pirouetting on his toes,
He kissed the lion's velvet nose.

"I knew I'd find you here," he said.
"Each night when I get into bed
I have the most exciting dream,
Where things are really what they seem.

"But, lion dear, I never knew
A dream as wonderful as you."
The lion smiled at Niccolby:
"And you're the sweetest dream for me."

All night they chatted happily,
The boy upon the lion's knee,
But when the sky was pink with dawn,
The lion gave a mighty yawn:

"Now if you climb into your bed
As soon as twilight's done," he said,
"And if I go to sleep by day
Then you and I can always play."

And so 'twas here he spent each nigh
And fell asleep in morning light
So he could dream of Niccolby
Beneath that happy willow tree . . .

When evening bells begin to chime,
There comes a slightly magic time
For little boys who've gone to bed
And tucked the covers round their head.

A time that offers privacy
And world enough for fantasy,
When shadows playing on the wall
Can be most anything at all.

A lion striped from head to toe
And gaily waltzing to and fro
Is partly dream and mostly true,
But then, perhaps, you always knew.